For Gabriel – C. F.

For Mum 'n' Pop – S. M.

Text copyright © 2008 by Claire Freedman
Illustrations copyright © 2008 by Simon Mendez
All rights reserved. Published by Scholastic Press, an imprint of Scholastic Inc.,
Publishers since 1920, by arrangement with Little Tiger Press, an imprint of Magi
Publications. SCHOLASTIC, SCHOLASTIC PRESS, and associated logos are
trademarks and/or registered trademarks of Scholastic Inc.

ISBN-13: 978-0-545-10568-2
ISBN-10: 0-545-10568-4

10 9 8 7 6 5 4 3 2 1   08 09 10 11 12

Printed in China
This edition first printing, September 2008

The text was set in 19-point Goudy.
The display type was set in Centaur Swash.

Book design by Kristina Albertson

On This Special Night

CLAIRE FREEDMAN   SIMON MENDEZ

SCHOLASTIC PRESS
New York

It was a silent winter's night. Little Kitten was snuggled up
in the old, wooden barn.

Outside, frosty trees glistened in the shadowy twilight.
High above, the heavens sparkled, watching, waiting. . . .

"Cuddle up closer," Mother Cat said. "Try and go to sleep."

"But the stars are so bright tonight," cried Little Kitten.

One star was bigger than the rest. Blazing with a brilliant light, it seemed to fill the heavens.

"That must be a special star," Mother Cat whispered.

Just at that moment, a gentle crackle of leaves broke through the stillness of the night.

"Could I trouble you for some water?" asked Donkey, nudging open the door. "I've been traveling all day and I'm thirsty."

"Of course," said Mother Cat kindly. "And you are welcome to stay in the barn with us tonight."

Donkey smiled. "Thank you," he said. "But I am on a very special journey." And he trundled out into the soft, silver moonlight.

Little Kitten watched, wondering. . . .

Just then Little Kitten heard a gentle *Baa! Baa!*

"I've walked such a long way," bleated Lamb, "and I'm oh so tired. Could I rest for a while in your soft hay?"

"Why, of course," said Mother Cat.

So Lamb curled up with his new friends, cozy, calm, and peaceful.

Outside, high in the sky, the biggest, brightest
star blazed on, watching, waiting. . . .
"Do you know why that star is so bright
tonight?" Little Kitten asked Lamb.

"Oh, yes!" whispered Lamb.
"I can tell you a story about that star. . . ."

But before Lamb could begin, there came a *Scritch!*
Scratch! Scritch! Scratch! and three tiny mice
peered through a crack in the wall.

"May we snuggle up with you?" they said, shivering.
"We've been walking forever, and our paws are frozen!"

"It's time I carried on my journey," Lamb said softly.
And silently he tiptoed away.

The mice nestled down, out of the bitter cold,
sharing the shelter of the snug, cozy bed.

"Where are you traveling to?" Little Kitten
asked. "Are you following the star?"

But before they could answer, there came
a *Moo! Moooo!* and Calf peeped his head inside
the battered door. Another visitor!

"Do you have any food to spare?" Calf asked. "I haven't had time to eat this evening."

There was plenty of fresh hay and Calf
chewed hungrily. "Thank you," he mumbled.
"I can't stay long; I must be on my way."
The mice stretched and yawned.
"We must hurry, too," they said.
"But where are you all
going?" Little Kitten cried.

Calf smiled, his big, brown eyes shining.
"Tonight is a very special night," he said.
"Something amazing is going to happen."
"Come with us — and you'll see it, too!"
squeaked the mice.

"Oh, can we?" Little Kitten shivered with excitement.

"We'll climb to the top of the barn roof," said Mother

Cat, "to see what we can see."

High on the roof, the air was crisp and
clear and cold. Little Kitten gazed in wonder at
the sparkling, starlit sky. It felt as if the whole world
were holding its breath, watching, waiting. . . .

"Look, Mama!" Little Kitten cried.

There, silhouetted against the dark night sky, walked
three magnificent camels.

"This is a *very* special night, Little Kitten!" Mother Cat whispered.

Shadows softened in the still night air as Mother
Cat and Little Kitten followed their friends to the
bottom of the hill. There stood a simple stable,
aglow in the light of the shining star.

Tenderly, Mother Cat helped Little Kitten squeeze inside the stable. His heart burst with happiness at what he saw: a baby! It was sleeping soundly in the sweet, soft hay.

This was a very special baby.

The animals watched quietly as, above them all, the bright, bright star blazed in the night . . . shining with peace

and joy

and love.